A Gift For:

Jack & Luke

From:

Kelley + Nate Clark

In loving memory of Hallmark master artist
Mary Hamilton, who inspired Mary's Angels,
loved painting and teddy bears, and looked
after her own wet kitten, Sniffles.

Published by Hallmark Gift Books,
a division of Hallmark Cards, Inc.,
Kansas City, MO 64141
Visit us on the Web at Hallmark.com.

Editorial Director: Delia Berrigan
Editor: Kim Schworm Acosta
Art Director: Chris Opheim
Designer: Brian Pilachowski
Production Designer: Dan Horton

ISBN: 978-1-63059-817-4
BOK1323

Made in China
0917

What Do Angels Do?

A MARY'S ANGELS STORY

BY Suzanne Berry   ILLUSTRATED BY Elizabeth Savanella

Hallmark

Angels are everywhere doing God's work
(though they like to stay just out of view).

But they're playful and kind, and leave little signs
to remind you they're smiling on you!

Each angel has special blessings to share.
Some even start every day with a song!
If you listen, you'll hear their joy in the air
as little birds twitter along!

Angels are silly! They giggle and play,
and jump on the clouds way up high!

They sculpt funny shapes and make "cloud angels," too,
which we sometimes can see in the sky!

Some angels tend to each wandering lamb,
wet kitten, and lost teddy bear.

They love all God's creatures—both great big and small—
and give them the cuddliest care.

We each have an angel who stays by our side
so we're never alone or apart.

Sometimes their wings softly stir up the breeze
and a flutter of peace fills our heart.

Angels encourage the good in us all
and help it to blossom and grow.

In fact, when they water their seedlings above,
we sometimes get sprinkled below!

And when a storm comes, they help color the sky
with a symbol of hope we can see.

It reminds us God's there to the ends of the earth
and shining on us faithfully!

Angels are always talking to God—
they know that He hears every prayer.

Like us, they pause to just say "hello,"
and give thanks for the blessings we share.

Some angels spread a glow wherever they go,
and at night they light every star.

Look up and you'll see their little lights shine—
they're with you wherever you are!

Yes, angels are everywhere doing God's work,
great helpers both here and above.
But whatever they do, know they're smiling on you
and surrounding you always with love.

Did you enjoy this Mary's Angels story?
We would love to hear from you.

Please write a review at Hallmark.com,
e-mail us at booknotes@hallmark.com,
or send your comments to:
Hallmark Book Feedback
P.O. Box 419034
Mail Drop 100
Kansas City, MO 64141